The Flow

Written by Jill Eggleton
Illustrated by Jim Storey

One day, a robber
looked over the fence.

"The beeman has flowers,"
said the robber.
"I will get over this fence.
I will get all his flowers."

3

The robber got over
the fence.

He went up to the flowers,
but the bees came out.

4

"**Help!**" said the robber.
"I can't get the flowers today."

And he ran away.

But . . . the robber
came back again.

The bees saw the robber
looking over the fence.
They went into the flowers
and they stayed inside.

The robber got
over the fence.

He looked at
the flowers.

"Good," he said.
"No bees!
I will get the flowers.
I will put them in this bag!"

But the bees came
out of the flowers.

They went
buzzz, buzzz, buzzz
on the robber.

11

"**Help!**" said the robber.

The robber put the bag down
and ran away.

The beeman put
a sign on his fence.

"The robber will not come
here again," he said.

An Action/Consequence Chart

Guide Notes

Title: The Flower Robber
Stage: Early (3) – Blue

Genre: Fiction
Approach: Guided Reading
Processes: Thinking Critically, Exploring Language, Processing Information
Written and Visual Focus: Action/Consequence Chart, Speech Bubbles, Thought Bubble

THINKING CRITICALLY
(sample questions)
- What do you think this story could be about? Look at the title and discuss.
- Look at the cover. What do you think the Flower Robber wants to do with the flowers? What might the bee be thinking?
- Look at pages 2 and 3. What do you think the bees would do if there were no flowers in their garden?
- Look at pages 8 and 9. Why do you think the robber is dressed in bright clothes? Focus on the brightness of his clothes and discuss camouflage.
- Look at pages 10 and 11. How do you think the robber is feeling? How can you tell he is feeling like this?
- Look at page 14. Look at the sign and discuss the word *bee-ware*. Why do you think the robber won't come back again?

EXPLORING LANGUAGE

Terminology
Title, cover, illustrations, author, illustrator

Vocabulary
Interest words: sign, robber, fence, bag, flowers
High-frequency words: one, day, ran, back, again, stayed, today
Positional words: over, inside, in, down, on, up, out, into
Compound words: beeman, inside

Print Conventions
Capital letter for sentence beginnings, periods, commas, exclamation marks, quotation marks, ellipsis